THE TWELVE DOGS OF CHRISTMAS

by Emma Kragen age 7

Tommy NELSON

Thomas Nelson, Inc.
Nashville

Photography by Donald Fuller • Illustration & Design by Sharon Collins & Kelly Ann Moore

Published in Nashville, Tennessee, by Tommy Nelson, a division of Thomas Nelson, Inc.
Managing Editor: Laura Minchew; Editor: Tama Fortner

Special thanks to: Poodle: Sara (Best Toy Poodle Puppy, "Poodle Club of America" 1997); St. Bernards: Disney & Xerxes; Cocker Spaniels: Whatzit (NA, OAJ), Whozit (CD, MX), & Kudos (CDX); Basset Hounds: Chuck (3rd in Hound Group, Clarksville 1995), Kate, Tillie (Best of Breed, Kentuckiana Basset Hound Specialty Show 1997), & Gracie (Best of Breed 1997, Clarksville Kennel Club Show); Golden Retrievers: Grace, Tipsy, Sunny, & Diana; Boxers: Be-Be (AKC Champion 1997), Jackie-O (Best of Breed and Group Winner 1995), Murphy (mother of Be-Be), & ZaZu (daughter of Jackie-O); Siberian Huskies: Tyler (AKC Champion 1995), Alex (Back-to-Back Best in Show, Bahama's Kennel Club 1995), Trey, & Bubba (AKC Champion 1998); Old English Sheepdogs: Bailey (Best in Show and Best in Group), Eliza (Best of Breed), Genna, & Rachel; Chihuahuas: Texas Kid, Davy Crockett, Dallas Kid, & Chiquita; Dalmatians: Winston (AKC Champion 1993 and Group Winner), Abby (AKC Champion 1998), Jerry (AKC Champion 1998), Summit (Future Champion), & Burnie; Chocolate Lab puppies: McKay, Mocha, Molly, & Samson.

Library of Congress Cataloging-in-Publication Data

Kragen, Emma.
    Twelve dogs of Christmas / by . . . Emma Kragen.
        p.   cm.
    Summary: An adaptation of the traditional English folk song, "The
Twelve Days of Christmas," featuring an increasing number of
different kinds of dogs instead of the usual gifts.
    ISBN 0-8499-5873-3
    1. Children's songs—Texts. 2. Children's writings. [1. Dogs—
Songs and music. 2. Christmas music. 3. Songs. 4. Children's
writings.] I. Twelve days of Christmas (English folk song)
II. Title.
PZ8.3.K857Tw   1998
782.42164'0268—dc21   98-38998
                                                           CIP
                                                           AC

Printed in the United States of America

99 00 01 02 03 WCV 9 8 7 6 5 4 3 2

I dedicate this book
to my dogs Angel and
Shadow for giving me the
idea for The Twelve Dogs
of Christmas.
Emma

On the **FiRST** day of Christmas, my true love gave to me...

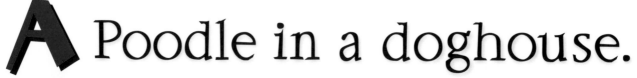
A Poodle in a doghouse.

On the **SECOND** day of Christmas, my true love gave to me,

2 St. Bernards...

And a Poodle in a doghouse.

On the **THiRD** day of Christmas, my true love gave to me,

3 Cocker Spaniels...

2 St. Bernards,

And a Poodle in a doghouse.

On the **FOURTH** day of Christmas, my true love gave to me,

4 Basset Hounds...

3 Cocker Spaniels,

2 St. Bernards,

And a Poodle in a doghouse.

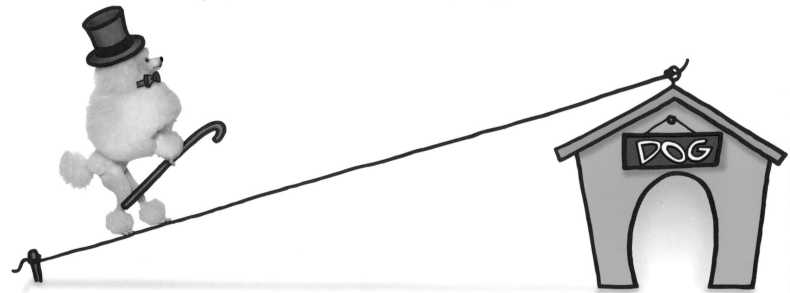

On the **FiFTH** day of Christmas, my true love gave to me,

 Golden Retrievers...

4 Basset Hounds,

3 Cocker Spaniels,

2 St. Bernards,

And a Poodle in a doghouse.

On the **SiXTH** day of Christmas, my true love gave to me,

6 Boxers boxing...

5 Golden Retrievers,

4 Basset Hounds,

3 Cocker Spaniels,

2 St. Bernards,

And a Poodle in a doghouse.

On the **SEVENTH** day of Christmas, my true love gave to me,

7 Huskies howling...

6 Boxers boxing,

5 Golden Retrievers,

4 Basset Hounds,

3 Cocker Spaniels,

2 St. Bernards,

DOG

And a Poodle in a doghouse.

On the **EiGHTH** day of Christmas, my true love gave to me,

8 Sheepdogs snoring...

7 Huskies howling,

6 Boxers boxing,

5 Golden Retrievers,

4 Basset Hounds,

3 Cocker Spaniels,

2 St. Bernards,

And a Poodle in a doghouse.

On the **NINTH** day of Christmas, my true love gave to me,

9 Chihuahuas chomping...

8 Sheepdogs snoring,

7 Huskies howling,

6 Boxers boxing,

5 Golden Retrievers,

4 Basset Hounds,

3 Cocker Spaniels,

2 St. Bernards,

And a Poodle in a doghouse.

On the **TENTH** day of Christmas, my true love gave to me,

10 Dalmatians dancing...

9 Chihuahuas chomping,

8 Sheepdogs snoring,

7 Huskies howling,

6 Boxers boxing,

5 Golden Retrievers,

4 Basset Hounds,

3 Cocker Spaniels,

2 St. Bernards,

A nd a Poodle in a doghouse.

On the ELEVENTH day of Christmas, my true love gave to me,

11 Labs a laughing...

10 Dalmatians dancing,

9 Chihuahuas chomping,

8 Sheepdogs snoring,

7 Huskies howling,

6 Boxers boxing,

5 Golden Retrievers,

4 Basset Hounds,

3 Cocker Spaniels,

2 St. Bernards,

 And a Poodle in a doghouse.

On the TWELFTH day of Christmas,
my true love gave to me...